Missy's
Super ♥ Duper ♥ Royal ♥ Deluxe

Class Pets

By
SUSAN NEES

BRANCHES
SCHOLASTIC INC.

For Maggie and her bright little Stars

No part of this work may be reproduced, stored in a retrieval system, or transmitted in any form or by any means, electronic, mechanical, photocopying, recording, or otherwise, without written permission of the publisher. For information regarding permission, write to Scholastic Inc., Attention: Permissions Department, 557 Broadway, New York, NY 10012.

Library of Congress Cataloging-in-Publication Data

Nees, Susan.
Class pets   by Susan Nees.
p. cm. -- (Missy's super duper royal deluxe ; 2)
Summary: Missy wants to take home the class pets, but another girl,
Tiffany, has already asked their teacher so Missy and her friend Oscar
need to come up with a plan to make Tiffany change her mind.
ISBN 978-0-545-43852-0 (pbk.) -- ISBN 978-0-545-49610-0 (hardback) --
ISBN 978-0-545-54010-0 (ebook) 1. Rats as pets--Juvenile fiction.
2.Elementary schools--Juvenile fiction. [1. Rats--Fiction. 2. Elementary
schools--Fiction. 3. Schools--Fiction.] I. Title.
PZ7.N384Cl 2013
813.54--dc23

                              2012035572

ISBN 978-0-545-49610-0 (hardcover) / ISBN 978-0-545-43852-0 (paperback)

12 11 10 9 8 7 6 5 4 3 2 1   13 14 15 16 17 18/0

Printed in China   38
First Scholastic printing, June 2013

Table of Contents

Chapter One
Pretty Please

This is Melissa Abigail Rose.

But everyone calls her "Missy."

This is Missy's cat Pink.

Everyone calls him "Pink."

Mornings are always busy for Missy. But today was extra busy. Today was special. Today Missy was going to bring home a class pet. Missy had to get everything ready. She made a sign.

She packed her lunch box.

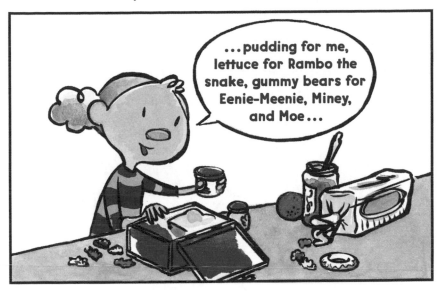

She helped Pink get dressed.

And most important of all, Missy fixed up her room. Her room needed to be ready. Ready for pets! Ready for fun! Ready for ACTION! Missy searched high and low, looking for what she would need.

On her shelves, she found a bottle of jumbo bubbles, an alarm clock, three rubber fish, one roller skate, and a map of Walla Walla, Washington.

Under her bed, she found a race car, a train set, a camera, a hula hoop, and an accordion.

In her closet,
she found...

an
umbrella,

a roll
of tape,

a tea set,

spy
glasses,

and a
flashlight.

Now everything was ready. Well, not quite everything. There was just one teeny-tiny thing left to do.

Missy had to ask her mother....

But Missy's mother said that the class pets would be noisy. And messy. And smelly.

And she said:

What if they were to get loose?

Missy's mother said NO. But Missy was not about to give up that easily.

Missy tried asking sweetly...

Pretty please with sugar on top?

slowly...

Pllleeeeaasssseee?

PLEASE!

loudly...

Please?!

Uh-oh.

She even tried standing on her head.

13

But still Missy's mother said no.

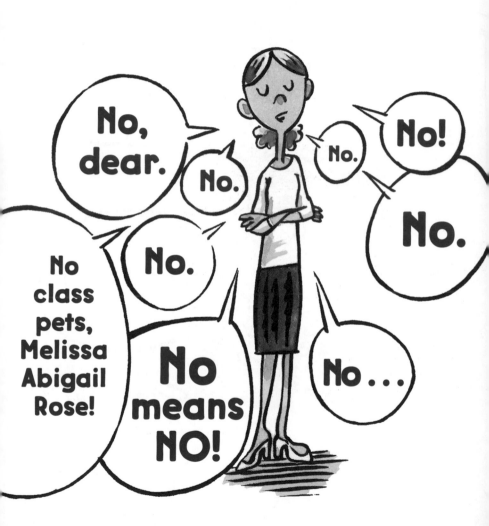

As she was leaving for school, Missy asked one last time.

Please, Mom? It's only for a few days, and they are soooooo cute and cuddly and sweet, and I PROMISE to take care of them!

This time, Missy's mother did not say no.

Chapter Two
Noodlehead

When Missy got to school, she was super duper excited to share her news.

At the end of the day, I get to choose a class pet to bring home. And I am going to choose Eenie-Meenie, Miney, and Moe. We are going to have a fashion show and a circus and a parade and a rodeo and ...

But before Missy could finish,
in walked trouble. Big trouble.
It was Tiffany. Tiffany was the
new girl. Tiffany was big. Tiffany
was loud. Tiffany had hairy arms.
But worst of all, Tiffany was mean.

29

Chapter Three
Oscar's Note

Missy's teacher, Miss Snodgrass, was a real stickler when it came to rules.

When class started, it was hard for Missy to concentrate.

Missy tried to listen. She really did.
But it was no use.

Rambo the snake
in a fashion show?
No way.

Mozart the goldfish
in a circus?
No!

Snickers the turtle in a parade?
Forget it!

George Washington the bird
in a rodeo?
Nope! Not happening!

Missy decided one thing was for sure—
she was going to need a plan.

She knew just who could help: Oscar.
Oscar was a thinker. Oscar would know
what to do.

Chapter Four
Green Gummy Bears

Missy was glad when it was time to go to the library. Missy liked the library.

It was a good place to think.

Hi, Oscar. What are you reading?

Shhh.

KARATE

But Oscar was no longer listening to Missy. Oscar was too busy thinking about facts.

47

Chapter Five
The Secret Plan

TICK...

TOCK...

TICK...

TOCK...

SIGH!

Missy could not wait for recess.
It seemed to take forever for the
bell to ring.

On the playground, Missy put her plan into action.

You can't catch me.

Yoo-hoo!

Tiffany! I have a secret.

Miss Mary Mack Mack Mack,

What do you want to do?

I don't know. What do you want to do?

Let's chase boys.

Chapter Six
Pet Parade

At the end of the day, Missy knew what was coming. And she didn't like it one bit.

Tiffany chose Eenie-Meenie, Miney, and Moe.
Taylor chose George Washington the bird.

The twins chose Snickers the turtle. Then
Paulette chose Rambo the snake.

And Missy got Mozart—the goldfish.

Hah!

Rats ran. Students screamed. Books flew and desks toppled. But that didn't stop Missy.

Don't worry! I'll take care of everything!

EEEEEEEKK!

Missy knew just how to find
Eenie-Meenie, Miney, and Moe.

Miss Snodgrass said Missy was a hero.
Miss Snodgrass said Missy could take
home any class pet she wanted. When
Missy chose Eenie-Meenie, Miney, and
Moe, no one was surprised.

And it was.

The End

Susan Nees

grew up on a farm, so she always had plenty of animals to play with. One hot summer day, Susan and her sister dressed up baby pigs in doll clothes and rigged up a blanket over the clothesline to serve as their "hospital." The sisters fed their "patients" green garden pea "pills." This went on until the piglets broke free, running across the yard trailing socks and bonnets. Today, Susan lives in Georgia with her family, Jodo the dog, and a small flock of chickens. Missy's Super Duper Royal Deluxe is Susan's first children's book series.

Class Pets

More
Super ♡ Duper ♡ Royal ♡ Deluxe
books!

#1

#2

#3

#4